CASPER
AND FRIENDS
BOO-O-S ON FIRST

By Stephanie St. Pierre
Illustrated by George Wildman

A GOLDEN BOOK · NEW YORK

Western Publishing Company, Inc., Racine, Wisconsin 53404

CASPER ™ AND FRIENDS TM & © 1992 Harvey Comics Entertainment, Inc..
All rights reserved. Licensed by MCA/Universal Merchandising, Inc. Printed in the U.S.A.
No part of this book may be reproduced or copied in any form without written permission from
the publisher. GOLDEN, GOLDEN & DESIGN, A GOLDEN BOOK, and A LITTLE GOLDEN BOOK
are registered trademarks of Western Publishing Company, Inc.
Library of Congress Catalog Card Number: 91-77590   ISBN: 0-307-00121-0

It was a sunny spring day. Casper the Friendly Ghost left the gloomy old house where he lived. He looked around for someone to play with.

"Gee—I wish I could find a friend," he said with a sigh as he flew above the town.

Casper soon came to a school where two crossing guards were waiting to help the children cross the street.

"This looks like a good place to find a friend," said Casper as he flew closer.

Casper landed right in front of the guards,
wearing his friendliest smile. "Hi!" he said brightly.

"Yikes!" yelled one guard.
"Help! A ghost!" yelled the other.
And they both dashed away down the street.

"Hey—wait a second!" Casper called after them.
But the guards were already far away.

"Gee," said Casper. "I only wanted to be friends."

Just then Casper heard the school bell ringing.
It was time for the children to be dismissed.

"Gosh, the children are going to need help crossing the street," said Casper. He was worried. Then he had an idea. "I guess I'll be their crossing guard today!"

Casper quickly put on one of the crossing guard's uniforms.

The children came to the crosswalk. They were so busy talking that they didn't notice Casper.

They all belonged to a baseball team called the Rockets. They were on their way to a big game.

"Hurry up, you guys," said a big boy carrying a baseball bat. "Let's get over to the park."

"Yes, let's get there before the Tigers so we can practice," said a girl on the team. She was tossing a ball into the air.

"Oops!" the girl cried as she dropped her ball.

The ball bounced away from her—and right through Casper!

"Don't worry. I'll get your ball," Casper told the
girl with a smile. He quickly flew after the softball.

Casper brought the ball back and held it out to the girl.

"Help! A ghost!" the kids screamed. They ran away as fast as they could, heading toward the park.

"Gee, I can't find anyone to play with today," Casper said sadly. "I guess I'll just go home."

Casper was about to fly away when he saw one
more little girl. She was all alone and looked unhappy.
"What's wrong?" Casper asked her.

"Oh, my!" the girl gasped when she looked up and
saw Casper. "You look like a ghost!"

"I'm a friendly ghost," Casper explained. "My name is Casper. What's your name?"

The little girl was scared, but she didn't run away. "My name is Jill," she said finally.

"Would you like to play ball with me, Jill?" said Casper.

Jill was quiet for a minute. Casper thought she might dash off, leaving him all alone again.

Then Jill smiled at Casper.

"Okay, Casper," she said. "Those other kids won't let me play with them. They say I'm too little. But I'll play with you."

"Great!" said Casper happily. Jill took his hand, and the two new friends walked over to the park.

Casper and Jill found a good place to play.

"Hey, that was a great catch!" said Casper when Jill caught a high fly ball. "Your turn to bat now."

"Sure," said Jill as they switched places. "This is fun!"

"Batter up!" Casper called out as he pitched the ball to Jill.

She swung hard and hit the ball. They both watched as the ball flew over a row of tall bushes.

"Great hit!" said Casper. Casper was about to fly after the ball. Then he said, "You'd better go get the ball, Jill. I don't want to scare anyone else today."

Jill ran after the ball and found the rest of the kids from school on the other side of the bushes. Her ball had landed right in the middle of the big game.

"You hit that ball way over here?" one boy asked her.

Jill just nodded.

"Hey, want to play on our team?" asked a girl on the Rockets.

"Sure!" Jill said. Then she remembered Casper. "I'll be right back," she told them.

Jill ran to the other side of the bushes and told Casper what had happened. "Come on, Casper," said Jill. "Let's play with the other kids."

"But I'll scare them all away," said Casper. "I always do."

Then Jill had an idea. "Can you make yourself invisible?"

"How's this?" said Casper with a laugh. He had disappeared completely.

"Perfect!" said Jill.

Jill stood in the outfield, ready to catch any balls that came in her direction. Casper was there, too. But nobody knew that except Jill.

"Casper . . . are you there?" she whispered. "I'm a little scared."

"Don't worry, I'll help you," Casper whispered back. Then he tugged playfully on her ponytail and made Jill giggle.

Finally it was the last inning. The Rockets were ahead by just one run. The next batter was the biggest boy on the other team. And the bases were loaded.

"Uh-oh," said Jill. "I bet this guy will hit the ball."

"But if we get him out, the Rockets win the game," said Casper.

"I hope so," Jill said nervously.

"Strike one!" called the catcher as the big boy swung and missed. The pitcher for the Rockets threw the next ball.

"Strike two!" called the catcher. One more strike and the game was over. The pitcher threw the ball, and the boy swung.

It was a hit. The ball soared into the blue sky.

"Oh, no!" cried Jill. It was going way over her head.

Jill ran back as fast as she could.

"You can do it, Jill!" called Casper, but he could see that she wasn't going to reach the ball in time.

Casper flew up, caught the ball, and dropped it right into Jill's glove!

"Hurray!" shouted the Rockets. "We won! We won!"
"And all because of you, Jill!" said one of the boys.
"But it wasn't just me. My friend Casper helped, too." Jill looked around, but Casper was still invisible. "Casper? Where are you?"

Suddenly all the kids could see Casper. But this time they didn't run away.

"Hurray for Jill and Casper!" they cheered.

"Come and play with us tomorrow," said a girl on the team. "You're great!"

Jill smiled at Casper, and he smiled back. They both knew they didn't have to worry anymore about making friends. They were Rockets now!